The Bus Home

Graeme Beals

PINNACLE PRESS

The Bus Home is the fifth in a five book series. Tom recovers and is ready to leave hospital. Will Tammy still want to be with him, once he is well again?

Titles follow in this sequence:

Tom and Tammy – The Bus Home
ISBN 9781906125455
Ordering Code – UK7000

Curriculum Concepts UK
The Old School
Upper High Street
Bedlinog
Mid-Glamorgan CF46 6SA

Email: orders@curriculumconcepts.co.uk
www.curriculumconcepts.co.uk

Illustrated by Ross Bennett

My leg is very sore.

x-ray

It was broken in two places.

To start I can't put it on the
ground.

My arm is not so bad though.

x-ray

It is only broken in one place.

Soon I can take it out of the sling.

It is in a plaster like my leg.

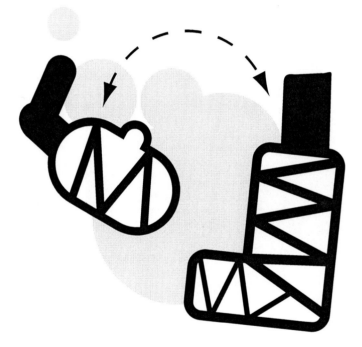

Each day Tammy comes to visit me.

I can't wait to see her.

She brings chocolates and grapes.

We share them while we talk
about things that happened that
day.

I slowly get better.

Soon I can walk with a crutch.

My head starts to feel better too.

At last the bandages start to come off.

I look in the mirror.

I have a scar on my forehead.

I think it makes me look strong.
I like it.

When Tammy comes she looks at the scar.

Then she touches it very gently.

"You poor silly thing," she says
and smiles. I think she like it too.

At last, they say I can go home.

Tammy comes to help me.

She carries my bag.

She puts her other arm around
me so I won't fall.

I like that.

We go to the bus stop.

She helps me onto the number 10.

We find a seat.

I think of when we first met.

"I like buses," I say, smiling at her.

"Me too," Tammy says and puts
her head on my shoulder.